Up Against the Wall

D1546264

By John Michlig
Illustrated by Art Mawhinney

A GOLDEN BOOK • NEW YORK
Western Publishing Company, Inc., Racine, Wisconsin 53404

In the Great Forest of the planet Mobius, the brave Freedom Fighters were listening to Antoine, their record keeper. "Dr. Robotnik and his Badniks have been quiet lately," he reported. "Maybe he's ready to give up!" said Tails, the two-tailed fox.

"No way," said Sonic the Hedgehog, lightning-quick leader of the Freedom Fighters. He knew that the evil Robotnik wouldn't stop until every living thing on the planet was destroyed or robotized.

Suddenly a BOOM shook the ground. "That sounds like thunder," said Bunnie Rabbot.

"But there isn't a cloud in the sky," said Rotor.

"Could be trouble," Princess Sally said.

"Sorry, Antoine, I'll see you later!" said Sonic, streaking away.

A few seconds later Sonic was outside Robotropolis. He was
stopped by a giant machine that was slamming pieces of metal
into the ground. BOOM! BOOM! BOOM!

The rest of the Freedom Fighters caught up to Sonic. They watched in horror as the machine scooped up trees.

Just then the evil Dr. Robotnik appeared with his assistant, Snively. "Welcome to my construction site," Robotnik called. "As you can see, the Wall-Upper 3000 is expanding Robotropolis."

"I knew you'd show your creepy face sooner or later," Sonic said. "Take your overgrown toy and go back inside Robotropolis!"

"Soon all of this *will* be Robotropolis," Robotnik said. "The Great Forest will be encircled with a giant metal wall. Then I'll put a huge dome over it to keep out the annoying sun." He demonstrated by covering a flower with his hat.

"Without sunshine all the plants and animals will die!" Sally said.

"Let's see how your bucket of bolts handles a Sonic Spin!" said Sonic, launching himself at the Wall-Upper 3000.
Sonic bounced off the machine. "Hey, that smarts!" he said.

"We won't let you kill the forest!" said Bunnie.

"My Swatbots and Buzzbombers will see to it that you don't interfere," Robotnik roared. Sure enough, they began to chase the Freedom Fighters.

"There's way too many of them!" Antoine said. "I suggest a hasty retreat."

Sally agreed. "Let's go home and come up with a plan!"

But Sonic wasn't ready to go. Sally had to drag him off.

The Freedom Fighters scrambled through a tunnel to the safety of their secret meeting hall in Knothole Village.

"My Sonic Spin didn't even dent that contraption," Sonic said.

"At least there's still time to get the forest animals out before they're trapped inside the wall," Antoine said.

"But the animals won't have any place to live," said Sally.

"Robotnik must be stopped!" Sonic told his friends.

For a while there wasn't a sound in the hall. Finally Sonic broke the silence. "I know how to scrap Robotnik's machine," he said. "But first we must get rid of Robotnik and the Swatbots."

"We could magnetize the metal wall with Rotor's giant magnet," said Sally. "Then the wall would become a supermagnet. When the metal Swatbots get too close—ZAP—they're stuck!"

"Great idea, Sally," Sonic said. Then he gathered paper, paints, and brushes. "Now we need Bunnie's artistic talent."

"Bunnie will draw some scenery that will trick the machine," Sonic explained. "When I bounced off it, I saw that its computerized eyes were following a route created by Robotnik. All we have to do is change the route."

Later that day Sonic, Antoine, and Sally pulled a chest of
Golden Rings—the bait they hoped would trap Robotnik—to
the Wall-Upper 3000.

Robotnik and Snively were busy making plans to robotize more of Mobius when they saw the Freedom Fighters approach.

"We want to make a deal, Robotnik," Sonic said. "If you stop building the wall, we'll give you this chest of Golden Rings."

"It could be a trick," Snively whispered to Robotnik.
"I'll be trickier," Robotnik whispered back.
Then he turned to Sonic. "Okay—it's a deal."

Robotnik and Snively quickly checked the chest for a trap.
"HA! The trick's on you, suckers!" Robotnik said. "I'll
just take the Golden Rings. Swatbots, attack!"

Robots appeared from everywhere. They surrounded the
Freedom Fighters and backed them against the wall.

"I know a better trick," Sonic said. Then he whistled.
At Sonic's signal Rotor popped out of the chest with the magnet. He flicked a switch and was pulled over to the wall.

As the wall became magnetized, Robotnik and his metal Badniks stuck to it! Then Sally dropped a net over the nonmetallic Snively.

"You may have tricked me, but you haven't stopped my machine," Robotnik cried while Sonic reclaimed the Golden Rings.

"Just watch," said Sonic as Tails darted in front of the machine and held the new route in front of its unblinking eyes.

Fooled by the pictures, the machine zigged left . . . and zagged right . . . then left again . . . until it toppled over a cliff.

Back at their village, the Freedom Fighters celebrated. They'd outsmarted Robotnik once again!

"By the way, Sally," Rotor said, "that magnet was a great idea."

"Well," said Sonic, it must have been my magnetic personality that inspired her."